For Margaret O'Kelly who taught me how to teach the children
of Wonderland Nursery School, Hollywood, California – *J.N.H*

For Margaret Crowden, a wonderful teacher – *J.N.H. and S.P.*

National Library of Canada Cataloguing in Publication

Hunter, Jana Novotny
I have feelings / Jana Novotny Hunter ; illustrations by Sue Porter.
-- Canadian ed.

ISBN 0-439-98980-9

I. Porter, Sue II. Title.

PZ7.H94lh 2002   j823'.914   C2002-901142-6

First published in Great Britain in 2001 by Frances Lincoln Limited

6 5 4 3 2 1   Printed in Singapore   02 03 04 05

I Have Feelings

Jana Novotny Hunter

Illustrated by Sue Porter

SCHOLASTIC CANADA LTD.

Everyone has feelings –
mummies, daddies, children –
even babies do!
Everyone has feelings...

...just like me and you.

Waking up is my best time.
I feel a laugh bubbling up
inside me. It comes out
on my face.

I'm feeling...

happy!

Uh-oh! Someone's not happy now.
My baby sister feels full up
with tears and she needs
to cry them out until
there are no more left.

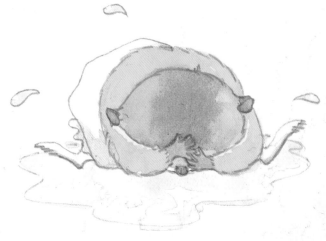

Baby's feeling...

"Want to watch me
dress myself?" I say.

"Look, I can do up
all my buttons."
The words are
bursting to come out.

I'm feeling...

Now that I'm dressed
we can go to the park.
"Hurry up, Mummy!

Hurry up!"

I'm feeling so
speedy-fast inside,
I just can't stop
jumping around.

I'm so...

excited!

But the bubbly feeling bursts when my baby sister gets to the big swing first.

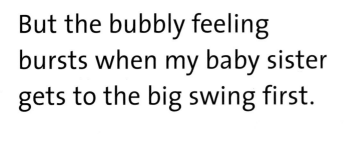

Wanting and *wanting* my turn is taking up all the room inside me.

Now I'm feeling...

It's hard to share.
And anyway, my baby sister
is too little for that swing,
so I have to help her.

And helping her
makes me *like* myself.

I'm feeling...

kind.

"I think it's time
we went home now!"
says Mummy.

"No! I don't want to!
I don't want to!"
I feel a shout growing
bigger and bigger inside
me and I have to
open my mouth wide
and let that shout go.

I'm feeling very...

Letting out the shout
helps the anger go away.
So when we get home
I'm better.

But at bedtime I get
all shivery inside.
Angry monsters are
coming and I need
them to leave me
alone.

They're making me feel so...

My daddy helps me chase those naughty monsters away.

I can feel a cuddle
coming down
my arms.

I snuggle up
and give it
to him.

I'm feeling...

And Daddy feels love right back!

Everyone has feelings –
mummies, daddies, children –
even babies do!

Everyone has feelings...

...just like me and you!

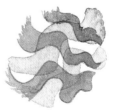